Every new generation of children is enthralled by the famous stories in our Well-loved Tales series. Younger ones love to have the story read to them. Older children will enjoy the exciting stories in an easy-to-read text.

Published by Ladybird Books Ltd Loughborough Leicestershire UK
Ladybird Books Inc Lewiston Maine 04240 USA

Hansel and Gretel

retold for easy reading
by JOAN CAMERON

illustrated by PAT OAKLEY of Hurlston Design

Ladybird Books

Once upon a time, there were two children, a boy called Hansel and his sister Gretel. They lived with their father and stepmother in a little cottage at the edge of a forest.

Their father was a woodcutter, and he was very poor. Once, he had so little money that he could not even give his family enough to eat. This made him very unhappy.

"How can we feed the children?" he asked his wife one night. "We have just enough for two, but not for four."

5

His wife did not really like the children. "Listen, husband," she replied. "I know what we must do. Tomorrow we will take the children into the thickest part of the forest. We will make a fire for them, and give them each a small piece of bread. Then we must leave them there. They will never find their way home. We shall be free of them!"

"I could never do that," said the woodcutter. "How can you even think of such a thing?"

"You fool!" his wife cried. "Then we will all die of hunger!"

And she gave him no peace, until at last he agreed.

Too hungry to sleep, Hansel and Gretel overheard what was said. Gretel cried bitterly.

"What shall we do?" she sobbed.

"Don't worry, Gretel," her brother said. "I will look after you."

Once his parents were asleep, he crept quietly outside. White pebbles lay around, like silver coins in the moonlight. He filled his pockets with them, and went back to bed.

Early next morning, the woodcutter's wife wakened the two children.

"Get up," she told them. "We are going into the forest to chop wood."

She gave them each a piece of bread.

"This is for your dinner. Don't eat it before then."

They all set out together. Hansel's pockets were full of pebbles, so Gretel carried their bread in her apron.

They had gone a little way when Hansel stopped, and looked back towards the house. After he had done this several times, his father spoke to him.

"Hansel, why are you lagging behind?"

"My white cat is on the roof, father," said Hansel. "I am trying to say goodbye."

"That isn't a cat, you silly boy," scolded his stepmother. "It's the sun, shining on the white chimney!"

But Hansel wasn't really looking at a cat. Each time he stopped, he dropped a pebble from his pocket on to the path.

They came to the middle of the forest. The woodcutter told his children to gather sticks.

"I will make a fire," he said. "Then you won't be cold."

Soon a fire was burning brightly.

"Rest here," their stepmother said. "We are going to chop wood. We will come for you when we are ready."

Hansel and Gretel sat by the fire. At noon, they ate their bread. They could hear the sound of an axe, and thought their father was near. But he wasn't. What they heard was only a branch, knocking against a tree trunk in the wind.

Hansel and Gretel waited so long that they fell asleep. When they woke, it was dark.

"What shall we do?" Gretel was frightened.

Hansel comforted her.

"Wait until the moon comes up," he said. "Then we will find our way home."

At last the moon rose in the sky. Hansel took his sister's hand, and followed the pebbles he had left on the path. They shone like silver coins in the moonlight, and showed the children the way home.

The children walked all night. As dawn came, they found their father's cottage, and knocked on the door.

Their stepmother opened it. "You naughty children!" she scolded them. "Where have you been? We thought you were never coming home!"

The woodcutter was very happy to see them. It had broken his heart to leave them in the forest.

Before long, the family had very little food again. One night the children heard their stepmother talking to their father.

"We have half a loaf left," she told him. "Once that is gone, we will have nothing. We must take the children deeper into the forest. This time they must not find their way home. It is the only escape for us!"

The woodcutter's heart was heavy. He would rather have shared his last crust with his children. But his wife would not listen to his pleading, and again he had to agree.

As soon as the woodcutter and his wife were asleep, Hansel got up, meaning to fill his pockets with pebbles as before. But his stepmother had locked the door. He couldn't get out. Sadly, he went back to bed.

"Don't cry, Gretel," he said bravely. "All will be well, you'll see."

Early next morning, the stepmother wakened the children. Before they left for the forest, she gave them each a very small piece of bread.

As they walked through the trees, Hansel bent down every now and then. Each time, he dropped a crumb of bread on to the path.

"Hansel, why do you keep stopping?" his father asked.

"I'm looking back at my little dove,"

Hansel replied. "He's nodding goodbye to me."

"You silly boy," the woodcutter's wife said scornfully. "That isn't a dove. It's the sun, shining on the chimney."

But as he went, Hansel still kept on dropping crumbs.

25

The woodcutter's wife led the children to a part of the forest they didn't know. Making a huge fire, she told them: "Stay here, by the fire. We're going into the forest to cut wood. We'll fetch you in the evening."

At noon, Gretel shared her small piece of bread with Hansel, for he had dropped all of his on to the path. Then they went to sleep. Evening arrived, and no one came.

"Don't be afraid, Gretel," Hansel told his sister as it grew dark. "When the moon comes up, we will see the crumbs of bread I dropped. They will lead us home."

Soon the moon shone, but they couldn't see any bread. The birds had eaten it all!

"We'll soon find the way," Hansel kept telling his sister.

But they didn't. They walked all night, and all next day, and they were still deep in the forest. They were so tired they could go no further, and lay down under a tree to sleep.

Next morning the children walked on. They were very hungry. By midday Hansel felt they must get help soon, or they would die of hunger.

Just then, a beautiful white bird perched on a nearby branch. It sang so sweetly that they followed it as it flew through the trees.

The bird led them straight to a little cottage!

"Look, Hansel!" cried Gretel. "The cottage is made of bread and cakes, and the windows are made of sugar!"

The two children ran forward.

"We'll have a feast," Hansel said. "I'll eat a piece of bread. You can try the cake!"

Hansel broke off a piece of bread, to see how it tasted. Gretel took a bite from one of the cakes. Soon they were both munching happily.

Just then, the door opened. Out came an old woman, walking on crutches. Hansel and Gretel were so frightened, they dropped what they were eating. But the old woman smiled at them.

"Come in, children! Stay with me, and you will come to no harm."

Taking them by the hand, she led them inside the little cottage. A meal of pancakes, milk and fruit lay ready on the table. In the back room were two little beds. After they had eaten, the children lay down, happy to be safe at last.

The old woman had been very kind to Hansel and Gretel. But they did not know that she was really a wicked old witch, who trapped children. She couldn't see very well, for witches have bad eyesight. But she had a fine sense of smell, as animals do. She could smell children coming.

The house of bread and cakes had been built to tempt children in. Once inside, the witch cooked them, and ate them!

Now that Hansel and Gretel were asleep in the little beds, the witch gave an evil laugh. "These two shall not escape!" she cackled.

Early next morning, the witch pulled Hansel roughly from his bed, and locked him in a cage. Although he screamed, there was no one to help him.

Gretel came next. The witch shook her awake.

"Get up, you lazy girl!" screeched the witch. "Cook something good for your brother. He will stay in that cage until he is fat enough for me to eat!"

The little girl began to cry, but the wicked witch only laughed at her tears. Gretel had to do what she was told.

Day after day passed. As the witch had hidden the key, Hansel had to stay in the cage. Gretel was soon tired out, for the witch made her clean and scrub, and cook huge meals for poor Hansel.

Every morning the witch went up to the cage.

"Hold out your finger, Hansel," she would cackle. "Let me feel if you are fat enough to eat."

But Hansel would hold out a bone instead. The witch had such bad eyesight that she always thought it was his finger. She wondered why it grew no fatter.

Four weeks passed. Because of Hansel's clever trick, the witch thought he was still very thin. She lost her patience.

"Fetch some water, Gretel!" she shrieked angrily. "This morning I will kill Hansel, and cook him."

The tears ran down Gretel's face, but the old witch made her fetch the water, and make a fire.

"First of all, we'll bake," the old witch said with a sly look at Gretel. "I have already made the dough, and heated the oven."

She pushed the little girl up to the oven door. Flames were burning fiercely around it.

"Go on," she said. "See if it's hot enough. Then we'll put the bread in."

But she really planned to put Gretel in the oven to bake. Then she would eat the little girl as well as Hansel.

Gretel had guessed what the wicked witch was thinking.

"I can't go in there," she said. "I'm too big."

"You silly child," the witch said angrily. "The oven is quite big enough. Look, I could even get in myself!"

She bent down, and put her head into the oven. Gretel gave her a hard push, and

she fell right inside. Shutting the iron door, Gretel bolted it.

The witch couldn't get out. The little girl ran away, leaving her there.

Gretel ran to Hansel's cage. "The witch is dead!" she cried. "We're safe! Now I must get you out of that cage."

Gretel couldn't find the key, so she broke the lock with a poker from the witch's own fireplace. The door swung open.

Hansel sprang out, like a bird from a cage. They hugged one another, over and over again.

Now they had nothing to fear. And when they looked over the witch's house, they found caskets of pearls and precious stones. "These are better than pebbles!" said Hansel.

He put as many into his pockets as they would hold. Gretel filled her apron.

"We must get out of this enchanted wood," Hansel told his sister.

They left the witch's cottage, and walked away through the trees. Hours later, they came to a large stretch of water.

"There's no bridge," Hansel said in

dismay. "We can't get over."

"There isn't a boat, either," Gretel said. "But, look, there is a white duck. I will ask her to help."

The duck agreed. She took them across the water on her back, one at a time, and soon they stood safely on the other side.

49

Hansel and Gretel had gone just a little way when they came to a part of the forest they knew. They began to run, and at last came to their own home. Inside, they ran into their father's arms. He had not had one happy moment since the children had been left in the forest. He was alone now, for their stepmother was dead.

"I'm so glad you've come home," he said.

Gretel shook out her apron, and pearls and diamonds rolled all over the floor. Hansel threw out one handful after another from his pockets.

Their troubles were over. From then on, the woodcutter and his children all lived happily together.